The
Pied Piper
of Hamelin

First published in 2007 by
Franklin Watts
338 Euston Road
London
NW1 3BH

Franklin Watts Australia
Level 17/207 Kent Street
Sydney
NSW 2000

Text © Penny Dolan 2007
Illustration © Martin Impey 2007

A CIP catalogue record for this book is available
from the British Library.

ISBN 978 0 7496 7075 7 (hbk)
ISBN 978 0 7496 7419 9 (pbk)

Series Editor: Melanie Palmer
Series Advisor: Dr Barrie Wade
Series Designer: Peter Scoulding

Printed in China

Franklin Watts is a division of Hachette Children's Books.

The
Pied Piper
of Hamelin

by Penny Dolan and Martin Impey

W
FRANKLIN WATTS
LONDON•SYDNEY

Once there was a rich town
where the people had plenty
of everything.

There were certainly plenty of rats
in the town! They stole food from
the dishes.

They made nests in every bed
and cupboard.

They fought the dogs ...

... and chased the cats!

The rats even bit the babies!

"You must get rid of the rats!"

the people told the Mayor.

So the Mayor put up a poster and
offered a reward to remove the rats.
The people waited and waited.

One day, a tall man appeared.
He was dressed in strange
clothes of different colours.

"I am the Pied Piper and I can get rid of your rats. But you must pay me a thousand gold coins," he said.

The Mayor whispered something to
his deputy. Then he spoke loudly:
"Piper, of course we will pay you
your reward."

As the Pied Piper stepped into
the street, he began to play a
magic tune. All the rats stopped
and listened.

The rats came running after the
Pied Piper. They ran faster and
faster.

15

The Piper stopped at the river,
but his music did not. Nor did
the rats.

They ran straight into the
rushing river, and that was
the end of them!

When the Pied Piper went to ask
for his reward, the Mayor laughed.
"You fool! The rats are gone now.
Take these few coins, and get out!"

The Piper was very angry.

"You will be sorry you broke

your promise to me," he said.

The Piper went out into the street.
He lifted his pipe to his lips,
and blew. At once, all the
children ran from the houses.

The children sang and danced, and laughed. They followed the Pied Piper's wonderful tune right out of the town.

Everyone was alarmed.

"Stop him! Pay him!"

they shouted at the Mayor.

"He cannot take them far,"
laughed the Mayor. "Look,
the mountain is in his way."

25

However, as the Pied Piper reached
the mountain, it opened up.

All the children followed the Piper and his music to a beautiful land.

Then the rocks closed. The children
and the Pied Piper were never seen
again. Only one poor child was
left outside the mountain.

Forever afterwards, the people
of that town were sad and silent.

How the Mayor wished he had
kept his promise!

Hopscotch has been specially designed to fit the requirements of the National Literacy Strategy. It offers real books by top authors and illustrators for children developing their reading skills. There are 43 Hopscotch stories to choose from:

Marvin, the Blue Pig
ISBN 978 0 7496 4619 6

Plip and Plop
ISBN 978 0 7496 4620 2

The Queen's Dragon
ISBN 978 0 7496 4618 9

Flora McQuack
ISBN 978 0 7496 4621 9

Willie the Whale
ISBN 978 0 7496 4623 3

Naughty Nancy
ISBN 978 0 7496 4622 6

Run!
ISBN 978 0 7496 4705 6

The Playground Snake
ISBN 978 0 7496 4706 3

"Sausages!"
ISBN 978 0 7496 4707 0

The Truth about Hansel and Gretel
ISBN 978 0 7496 4708 7

Pippin's Big Jump
ISBN 978 0 7496 4710 0

Whose Birthday Is It?
ISBN 978 0 7496 4709 4

The Princess and the Frog
ISBN 978 0 7496 5129 9

Flynn Flies High
ISBN 978 0 7496 5130 5

Clever Cat
ISBN 978 0 7496 5131 2

Moo!
ISBN 978 0 7496 5332 3

Izzie's Idea
ISBN 978 0 7496 5334 7

Roly-poly Rice Ball
ISBN 978 0 7496 5333 0

I Can't Stand It!
ISBN 978 0 7496 5765 9

Cockerel's Big Egg
ISBN 978 0 7496 5767 3

How to Teach a Dragon Manners
ISBN 978 0 7496 5873 1

The Truth about those Billy Goats
ISBN 978 0 7496 5766 6

Marlowe's Mum and the Tree House
ISBN 978 0 7496 5874 8

Bear in Town
ISBN 978 0 7496 5875 5

The Best Den Ever
ISBN 978 0 7496 5876 2

ADVENTURE STORIES

Aladdin and the Lamp
ISBN 978 0 7496 6678 1 *
ISBN 978 0 7496 6692 7

Blackbeard the Pirate
ISBN 978 0 7496 6676 7 *
ISBN 978 0 7496 6690 3

George and the Dragon
ISBN 978 0 7496 6677 4 *
ISBN 978 0 7496 6691 0

Jack the Giant-Killer
ISBN 978 0 7496 6680 4 *
ISBN 978 0 7496 6693 4

TALES OF KING ARTHUR

1. The Sword in the Stone
ISBN 978 0 7496 6681 1 *
ISBN 978 0 7496 6694 1

2. Arthur the King
ISBN 978 0 7496 6683 5 *
ISBN 978 0 7496 6695 8

3. The Round Table
ISBN 978 0 7496 6684 2 *
ISBN 978 0 7496 6697 2

4. Sir Lancelot and the Ice Castle
ISBN 978 0 7496 6685 9 *
ISBN 978 0 7496 6698 9

TALES OF ROBIN HOOD

Robin and the Knight
ISBN 978 0 7496 6686 6 *
ISBN 978 0 7496 6699 6

Robin and the Monk
ISBN 978 0 7496 6687 3 *
ISBN 978 0 7496 6700 9

Robin and the Friar
ISBN 978 0 7496 6688 0 *
ISBN 978 0 7496 6702 2

Robin and the Silver Arrow
ISBN 978 0 7496 6689 7 *
ISBN 978 0 7496 6703 0

FAIRY TALES

The Emperor's New Clothes
ISBN 978 0 7496 7077 1 *
ISBN 978 0 7496 7421 2

Cinderella
ISBN 978 0 7496 7073 3 *
ISBN 978 0 7496 7417 5

Snow White
ISBN 978 0 7496 7074 0 *
ISBN 978 0 7496 7418 2

Jack and the Beanstalk
ISBN 978 0 7496 7078 8 *
ISBN 978 0 7496 7422 9

The Three Billy Goats Gruff
ISBN 978 0 7496 7076 4 *
ISBN 978 0 7496 7420 5

The Pied Piper of Hamelin
ISBN 978 0 7496 7075 7 *
ISBN 978 0 7496 7419 9

* hardback